The Case of the
Disappearing
Kidnapper

(A Cody Smith Mystery)

by Dorothy Francis

D1111602

Cover and Inside Illustrations: William Ersland

About the Author

Dorothy Francis has written many books and stories for children and adults.

Ms. Francis holds a bachelor of music degree from the University of Kansas. She has traveled with an all-girl dance band, taught music in public and private schools, and served as a correspondence teacher for the Institute of Children's Literature in Connecticut.

She and her husband, Richard, divide their time between Marshalltown, Iowa, and Big Pine Key, Florida.

Printed in the United States of America. For information, contact

Perfection Learning® Corporation

1000 North Second Avenue, P.O. Box 500

Logan, Iowa 51546-0500

Phone: 800-831-4190 • Fax: 712-644-2392

PB ISBN-10: 0-7891-5260-6 ISBN-13: 9780-7891-5260-2

RLB ISBN-11: 0-7807-9657-8 ISBN-13: 9780-7807-9657-7

Printed in the U.S.A.

7 8 9 10 11 12 PP 14 13 12 11 10 09

Table of Contents

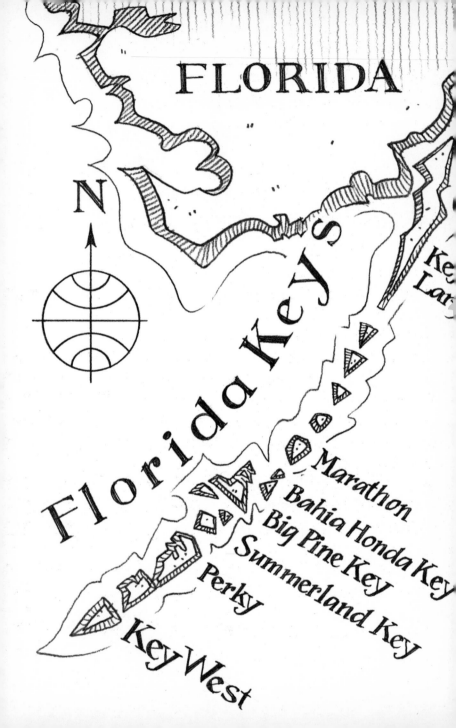

1

The Warning

My name is Cody Smith. I used to live in New York City. And I lived in Iowa with Gram for a while. But right now, Mom, Maria, and I are driving to the Florida Keys.

The Keys are small islands. They're like giant green stepping-stones between Miami and Key West.

"Are we almost there?" Maria asked. She pushed her radio headphones aside. Then she blew her curly black bangs from her forehead.

Maria fanned herself with her notebook. She called it her secret journal. She wanted to be a news reporter someday.

"Yes," Mom answered her. "Key West. Five miles ahead."

I sighed. Maria has bugged Mom with that question a lot. A whole lot. But I wanted the answer too. I'm tired of riding.

"It's been a long trip from Iowa," I said.

"Right," Mom agreed. "When we reach Key West, I'll need your help."

"Doing what?" I asked. I had been lying on the backseat. Now I sat up.

I ran my hand over my stubby red hair. Did red hair make a guy feel hot? Hotter than dark hair like Maria's? Or blond hair like Mom's?

"I'll need help finding Blossom Street," Mom said. "We're lucky my friend asked us to house-sit while she's away."

"Blossom Street sounds neat," Maria said.

Maria lived with us this summer. Her folks were working in Italy. They were paying us to watch her for the summer.

Maria was loud. And sometimes she was bossy. But I liked her.

She was good at keeping secrets. She's also good at solving mysteries. She used to shout out pretend headlines for articles she might write. But she'd stopped doing that now.

Instead, she wrote weird article ideas in her secret journal. Sometimes I peeked.

Yesterday she wrote . . .

Cat urine glows under black light.

Gross! But did it? I wondered. If I asked, she'd know I peeked.

Another time she wrote . . .

There are 178 seeds on a sesame seed bun.

How did she know that stuff? I thought she probably made it up.

"Mom," I said. "Someday I want to be a detective like you."

"Go for it," Mom said. "You can be whatever you want to be. But remember this. Caution is a good thing in a detective."

Caution? I'm always cautious. Well . . . most of the time.

"A *famous* detective, I suppose," Maria said.

Maria was teasing. I don't say much about fame anymore. Dad dumped Mom and me last year. I thought if I was famous, he might come home.

I wanted to get my name in *The Guinness Book of World Records*. I tried to wear the same Band-Aid for 100 days. But I took it off after only three days.

Then I tried to find Bigfoot in New York City. Bad thinking. But Maria and I did get our names in the paper.

But Dad didn't call. He didn't come home. I've given up on him. Too bad, Dad. You lost a neat family.

In Iowa, I saw bronze historical markers. And I set a new goal. I wanted to do something worthwhile. Worthwhile people got their names on bronze markers.

But that didn't work out either. I've put the bronze-marker idea behind me. I have a new plan.

"Maria, I've decided to be an eponym," I said.

Maria rolled her brown eyes. "What's an ep-o-nim? Spell it for me."

"E-p-o-n-y-m." She wrote *eponym* in her journal. I liked that. It made me feel special.

"An *eponym* is a person who gives his name to something important," I said.

"Oh sure." Maria used her I-don't-believe-you tone. "Show me an example."

I was prepared. I've read about eponyms. "Consider George Washington Ferris. He thought of turning a merry-go-round on its edge. And adding swinging seats. He invented the Ferris wheel. People say his name a lot. Being an eponym is a low-key way to fame."

"Low-key has never been your thing," Maria said.

"I'll work on it," I said. I imagined people saying, "He's a regular Cody Smith." That would mean "he's a great detective."

I didn't say that to Maria. But I mentioned Mr. Graham who invented the graham cracker. And I told her about Mr. Sax who invented the saxophone. They were low-key and subtle, but famous. That's what I wanted to be.

We crossed a long bridge and entered Key West. I inhaled the salt-scented air. I like to fill my lungs with good smells.

"On your left is the Atlantic Ocean," Mom said. "The Gulf of Mexico is on your right. Key West is about two miles wide and four miles long." She turned right. "Now help me find Blossom Street."

"Kennedy. Margaret. Caroline." I read some street signs.

"There!" Maria shouted after a long time. "Blossom."

It bugged me when Maria saw stuff first. But this time it was okay. I was just glad we had arrived.

Mom turned onto Blossom. The street grew narrow as a shoestring. But there were jillions of flowers.

"Just look!" Mom said. "Hibiscus. Alamanda. Bougainvillea. And I think that lavender flower is an orchid."

She stopped the car at a two-story house on a postage-stamp lot.

"Can't park there, lady," a truck driver shouted. "Use the driveway."

Mom did that. And the truck drove on. We looked at the house.

"Wow!" I said. "It needs paint."

"Some people here let their houses weather," Mom said. "They're built from a special kind of pine. I like its silvery look."

"I like the purple house next door better," Maria said. "And look at the pink one with the yellow shutters. Neat!"

I stubbed my toe. Tree roots poked through the sidewalk. Mom called them banyan roots. She said it was a kind of fig tree. Closer to the house, palm fronds cast dark fingers of shadow.

"This is one spooky place," I said. "I'll bet there are mysteries to solve here."

"First we unpack," Mom said.

We carried suitcases to the porch. Mom opened the door with a slim black key. We stepped into a square living room. There wasn't any carpet. But a sagging couch and three beanbag chairs looked cool. Beyond them, we saw a kitchen and a back porch.

"Upstairs first," Mom said.

I sneezed. The house had a closed-up-for-a-long-time smell. I took shallow breaths. I didn't want that smell messing up my lungs.

Upstairs we found a second-floor porch. And there were three bedrooms and a bathroom.

Mom raised windows. Cooler air blew in. She cranked open some ceiling hatches. Hot air swished out. I breathed again.

I chose the blue room. Mom chose green. And Maria chose lavender.

A tiny brown lizard sat on Maria's windowsill. At first it looked like a toy. But it darted away when we tried to touch it.

"They're called geckos," Mom said. "They're harmless."

Lizards in the bedrooms! Yuck! But I kept quiet. Maybe Florida Keys detectives learned to ignore lizards.

We tested the beds. They were soft. Lumpy, but soft. Then we hung our clothes on the bent hangers in the closets.

At last we went back downstairs. Mom plugged in the refrigerator and it hummed. Good!

"Grocery shopping's next," Mom said. She started a list. But just then someone knocked.

"Anyone home? I'm Rosa Sanchez from across the street."

Rosa's voice sounded low and reedy—like a bassoon. I peeked as Mom answered the door. Rosa wore her sleek black hair in a bun. A gold hoop earring dangled from her right ear. A silver hoop earring dangled from her left ear.

Did she know her earrings didn't match? She wore a sea-blue caftan and sandals. Gold bracelets jangled from her right wrist to her elbow.

I liked her immediately. Gypsy, I nicknamed her. I liked to nickname people. And she reminded me of a gypsy.

"Hello," Mom said. "I'm Gwen Smith. This is my son, Cody, and our friend, Maria. We're house-sitting for Sally West. Please come in."

"I won't bother you with company right now," Gypsy said. "I've come to warn you. Police think a kidnapper may be at large. Someone tried to take Angela Gomez. She lives next door. Keep a close watch on your children."

2

Angela's Tall Tale

"Please come in," Mom said. "We need to know more about this." She held the screen door open. I hoped another gecko wouldn't slither in with Gypsy.

Gypsy stepped inside. She eyed the beanbag chairs. Then she sat on the couch.

"It happened two days ago," Gypsy said. "At the beach. Of course, people don't believe everything a six-year-old says. But one never knows."

"What six-year-old?" Mom asked. "What did she say?"

"Angela Gomez," Gypsy said. "She lives next door in the purple house. She said a stranger offered her a yo-yo. She knew she shouldn't talk to strangers. But she loves toys. So she went with him. Then he grabbed her wrist, but she escaped."

"Thank goodness for that," Mom said. "Was she hurt?"

"No," Gypsy said. "The police came. But they doubted Angela's story. They searched the beach. Then they searched here. They didn't see any strangers that matched Angela's description."

"Did they find the yo-yo?" I asked. "It might have fingerprints on it."

Gypsy shook her head. "No yo-yo."

"Did Angela say what the man was wearing?" Mom asked. "Maybe he was in disguise."

Mom's always interested in disguises. Store detectives wore disguises when they watched for shoplifters.

"Angela couldn't remember exactly what he wore," Gypsy said. "She just said shorts and a T-shirt. But it's hot here. Lots of men dress like that. I don't mean to frighten you. I just thought you should know. And take care."

"Thank you," Mom said. "I'll keep a watchful eye on these kids. We're going out now for groceries."

"Be sure to come to Mallory Dock later this evening," Gypsy said. "People gather there to watch the sunset. I'll be selling key lime candy. You'll see lots of buskers there too."

"Buskers?" I asked. Maria jotted the word in her journal.

"Buskers are street performers," Gypsy said. "They arrive from all around the world. Come to the dock. You'll see some good acts."

Then she looked at Mom again. "Just watch these kids. A kidnapper could easily mingle with the sunset crowd."

I wanted to talk more with Gypsy. But she hurried off. Her house was orange with green shutters. Neat!

"I saw a small grocery store nearby," Mom said. "We'll shop there today. Tomorrow we'll hunt for a supermarket."

Mom & Pop's Grocery was hot and crowded. Besides us and Mom and Pop, three others were shopping. None looked like kidnappers.

Sometimes Maria and I helped make supper. I did grilled cheese sandwiches. Maria did salads. She also made pizzas with biscuit-dough crust. But Maria was best at making salads. And fruit cups.

But tonight Mom decided to cook dinner. She

made grilled chicken and broccoli. Afterward, I saw Maria write in her journal. I peeked.

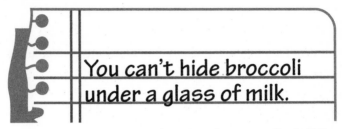

You can't hide broccoli under a glass of milk.

Mallory Dock was close by. So we walked. What noise! It was like a circus. A bagpiper showed off his talent for loudness. Dogs barked. Kids laughed and yelled.

Mom held my hand. I hated that. Jeepers! I'm almost 13! She held Maria's hand too. We looked at each other and rolled our eyes.

I tried to watch for the kidnapper. But the buskers distracted me. I forgot about kidnappers.

A crowd gathered around a tightrope walker. He wore a tank top, short shorts, and gold ballet slippers. A red ribbon held back his ponytail.

"Go, Will, go," a man shouted. Will didn't answer.

Wow! One misstep and he'd hit the concrete. Or splash into the harbor. Will inched across the rope. He juggled three tennis balls. Then he jumped down safely.

Everyone clapped and cheered. He passed around a hat, and most people tossed in a dollar.

Mom bought key lime candy from Gypsy. She wore a lime-colored caftan that matched her candy.

But her earrings still didn't match. Maybe mismatched earrings were her trademark. I liked them. And I liked the tart-sweet taste of her candy.

"Have you seen anyone who looks like a kidnapper?" I asked Gypsy.

"No," she said. "But I've been busy selling candy. Take care."

We watched a man perform with trained cats. I remembered Maria's article idea about cats. Too bad she didn't have a black light with her. Then we watched a Houdini-type guy wiggle from a straightjacket.

Enough! We'd had a long day. We went home to bed. I thought about the gecko. But even that didn't keep me awake.

The next morning after breakfast, Mom left us alone. She had to see about her job. We were almost 13. Mom thought our being alone was okay. I agreed.

"Don't talk to strangers," she called as she drove off.

"Maria," I said. "I see a little kid next door. It's probably Angela. Let's wander over and talk to her."

"We could ask her about the kidnapper," Maria said.

"Right," I said. "She may know more than she told the police. I'd like to find that kidnapper."

"You just want to be an eponym," Maria said. " 'He's a regular Cody Smith.' That's what you want people to say. You'd want it to mean 'he's a great detective.' "

Sometimes Maria could read my mind. "Catching a kidnapper would be a worthwhile thing, Maria. If it makes me an eponym, well, okay." I pretended not to care one way or the other. But I cared.

We walked to Angela's house. She was sitting on her porch playing jacks.

"Hi, Angela," I said. "I'm Cody, a detective. Maria's a writer. Will you tell us about the kidnapper?"

Angela's mother came to the door.

"Hello, children," she said. "We saw you move in yesterday. You're welcome here. But Angela's not to leave this yard."

"Thank you, Mrs. Gomez," I said. "We just came over to meet her."

Mrs. Gomez went back inside.

"Angela," I began again. "What can you tell us about the kidnapper?"

At first I thought she wasn't going to talk. She picked up her jacks and her ball.

"He was tall," Angela said.

I sighed. Anyone would look tall to a six-year-old.

"Where did you meet him?" Maria asked. She opened her journal, ready to write.

"On the beach," Angela said.

"Where was your mother?" I asked.

"At the food place," Angela said. "She was buying limeades."

"What did the man say?" I asked.

"He said he'd give me a yo-yo," Angela said. "He wanted me to walk to his car. That's where he kept his yo-yos."

"And you went?" Maria asked.

Angela nodded.

I wanted to know more, but Angela's story was spooking me out.

3

The Blue-Paint Clue

I had more questions for Angela. But her mother came outside again. I was afraid she might not want us prying. So I stopped asking questions.

But then Mrs. Gomez asked me to please go on. She wanted to hear Angela repeat her story.

"I wasn't scared at first," Angela said. "He was a nice man. He smiled. And he smelled like chocolate candy."

"What happened when you went with him?" I asked.

"He walked fast," Angela said. "I couldn't keep up. So he grabbed my wrist and pulled. I still couldn't keep up. The sand scrunched between my toes."

"So was he dragging you?" Maria asked.

"Sorta," Angela said. "Then we stopped for a minute. He pulled a blue yo-yo out of his pocket. And he gave it to me."

"Where is it?" I asked.

"I dropped it," Angela said. "I tried to stop and pick it up. I wanted that yo-yo. But he wouldn't let me. So I tried to get him to let go of me. I hated walking so fast."

"But he wouldn't slow down?" I asked.

"No," Angela said. "He pulled me to a bad part of the beach. I don't like to go there."

"Why is it a bad part?" I asked.

"There are no people there," Angela said. "Just big rocks and sand. And smelly seaweed. It's a scary place. But he pulled me there. And then the wind started to blow."

Angela took a breath and continued, "Sand hurt my cheeks. It got in my eyes. I tried to get away again. But he held me so tight I began to cry."

Angela's mother hugged her.

Angela turned back toward Cody and Maria. "I yelled for help," she told them.

"Did anyone hear you?" Maria asked.

Angela shrugged. "I'm not sure," she said. "I think someone came. But sand stung my eyes. I couldn't see."

"That's when I found her crying," Angela's mother said. "I didn't see any man. No yo-yo either. Angela's not supposed to go to that part of the beach. Maybe she made up this story to keep from getting in trouble. Or maybe her imagination was working overtime."

Poor Angela. It was tough that nobody believed her. Our friend, Mrs. Sugarman, said she saw Bigfoot in Central Park. Nobody believed her. I felt sorry for her too.

"You called the police?" I asked Angela's mother.

"No," Mrs. Gomez said. "Her crying attracted attention. A crowd arrived with a policewoman. She listened to Angela. But she didn't see any man either. She said we should take care. Just in case. You kids be careful too. Don't wander off alone."

"We'll be careful," I said.

Mrs. Gomez left. Angela pouted. "It wasn't my imagination," she said. She held out her hand. "See?"

Blue marks stained her fingers. "What's that?" I asked.

"It's paint from the yo-yo," Angela said. "But Mom

doesn't believe that either. She says the blue came from a marker."

"We believe you, Angela," I said. "We have to go home now. So you be careful. Don't talk to strangers."

"Okay," Angela said. Now she smiled at us. "You and Maria are my friends."

When we reached our house, Maria said, "She likes us because we said we believed her."

"But I do believe her," I said. "A little kid couldn't invent such a neat story. All those details. Would she make up a chocolate smell? Would she make up sand hurting her cheeks?"

"You may be right," Maria said.

"I think it really happened," I said. "I'm going to find that kidnapper. It'll be my first detective case here in the Keys."

"Better not tell your mom," Maria said. "She won't let you do dangerous stuff."

"You'll help me, won't you?" I asked. "It could make an awesome story for your journal."

"Sure," Maria said. "I'll help. But here comes your mother now."

We spent the rest of the day helping Mom with her disguises. I like disguises. Mom showed us a new wig. And a bag of really weird stuff.

"I start my job at noon tomorrow," Mom said. "I'm working for the Duval Street Merchants Association. Duval is the main street through Key West. I'm to go from store to store acting like a shopper. A tourist shopper. Of course, I'll be looking for shoplifters."

"Does a tourist look different from a regular shopper?" Maria asked.

"Sometimes," Mom said. "Tourists sometimes dress differently than local shoppers. And often they're carrying a camera to take pictures of their vacation. Some look confused because they aren't sure where they're going."

We followed Mom upstairs. She had lots of wigs. Her curly orange one looked like a pot scrubber. Her gray wig made her look 100 years old. Her black wig made her look like a TV star. But this new wig was different.

"Try it on," Maria said. "Let's see how you look in it."

The wig was a long-billed fishing hat. A scraggly brown ponytail hung from the back of it.

Mom put on sunglasses. Then she pulled the hat low on her forehead. We hardly recognized her.

"May I try it on?" Maria asked. Mom handed it to her.

"It looks cool on you too, Maria," I said. We all laughed. Disguises were a fun part of being a detective.

Mom tried on a false nose that made her look ugly. It was hard for Mom to look ugly. She taped on eyebrows that looked like brown caterpillars. Then she tried on a long dress and some necklaces. And shorts with a halter top. She modeled her disguises for us.

"I can't imagine blending into a crowd with these things," I said.

"Wait until you see the crowds," Mom said. "Key West is a do-your-own-thing place. I'll never be noticed. Believe me! By the way, I've got news."

"What?" Maria and I both asked at once.

"Before work tomorrow, we'll ride the Conch Train," Mom said.

"*Conk*? Like a conk on the head?" Maria asked.

"Yes, conk," Mom said. "That's how Key Westers pronounce *conch*. The Conch Train is a tourist attraction. It carries tourists all around the island."

"And we're going to ride on it?" I asked.

"Yes," Mom said. "The driver points out places of interest. The oldest house. The southernmost point. The Lighthouse Museum. Key West has many special places. And I want you to know about them."

My heart dropped to my toes. Who needed a history lesson? I wanted to hunt for a kidnapper.

4

The Conch Train

Mom made supper. She fixed grilled grouper. I didn't want any until she explained what it was.

I'd had enough weird food at Gram's in Iowa. Gram tested her cookbook recipes on us. She had a lot of strange recipes. I try never to think about it.

The Conch Train

"A *grouper's* a fish," Mom said. "I bought it today at the fish market."

The grouper tasted good—a little like chicken. I baked potatoes in the microwave. Maria made fruit salad with lots of orange slices and bananas. The fruit grew on trees in our yard.

After supper, Gypsy came over. She was wearing the same earrings, bracelets, and lime caftan as yesterday. But she didn't come inside.

"I just wanted to tell you about day camp," she said. "It's for kids 12 to 14 years old. I think you two kids would like it. And it's free. It's sponsored by the city."

"What do the kids do?" I asked.

"Crafts," Gypsy said. "Art. Writing. You get to choose what you'll do. It's fun. And it's well supervised."

"Where is it held?" Mom asked.

"Just a few blocks from here," Gypsy said. "Sea View Park." She gave us directions. "It's easy to find, and you'll be welcome." She waved good-bye as she hurried home.

That night, we didn't go to Mallory Dock. Instead, we stayed home to watch the blue moon. Mom said blue moons didn't happen often. It was when two full moons appear in the same month.

There was a widow's walk on our house. It was like a small porch on the rooftop. You reached it by climbing narrow stairs in my closet. And opening a trap door in the ceiling.

Long ago, women watched the ocean from widow's walks. They hoped to see their husbands' ships sailing home.

We climbed to the widow's walk. Mom went first to make sure it was safe. Then Maria. Then me. What a deal!

"Awesome," I said. "We're standing above the treetops. I feel like a giant looking over my kingdom. A kingdom of treetops and ocean."

"What about those high-rise hotels?" Maria asked. "They sort of spoil the view."

"I'm pretending they're not there," I said. "I'm imagining olden times."

We watched moonlight silver the banyan leaves. It shimmered against palm fronds. The wind in the palms sounded like rain. But the night looked clear.

Mom went back downstairs. But Maria and I stayed on the roof a long time. I liked the sweet, salty smell of sea air.

That night, I forgot about geckos on the windowsills. And kidnappers. Mom says live and let live. That's going to be my motto too—except for kidnappers.

The next morning we got up early. The air already felt hot as a steam bath. But right after breakfast we walked to Old Town. Mom bought tickets for the Conch Train.

Then I saw it coming. It was yellow and black. A jeep pulled a bunch of open-air cars. Rows of seats filled each car. And a roof shaded the passengers.

We climbed aboard, and the driver blew the horn. It had a loud GET-OUT-OF-MY-WAY sound.

"How long is this ride?" I asked. I hoped it would be short.

"An hour," Mom said. "Maybe longer."

I sighed. Maria rolled her eyes. But she had her journal ready.

I could see the last page.

> Pound for pound,
> hamburgers cost more
> than new cars.

Could that be true? I sighed again. Maybe someday I'd figure it out.

Mom sat by Maria. Nobody sat on the seat beside me. A boy about my age boarded the train alone. He looked like he'd be fun. So I motioned to the empty seat.

He saw me. But he sat in the back row instead. Maybe he didn't like my looks.

Our driver spoke into a microphone. "I'll give you a bit of Old Island history," she said.

I turned my ears off. It was going to be a long hour. But then I heard the word *Indian*. I turned my ears on again. I liked Indian stuff.

"The Calusa Indians lived here first," the guide said. "Then enemies arrived and killed them. The enemies left without burying the Indians' bodies. Later, Spanish gold hunters arrived. But they only found bones. They called the island *Cayo Hueso*. That meant Bone Key."

"So how did it get named Key West?" Maria called out.

"Say *Cayo Hueso* real fast," the guide said. "It sounds like Key West. Key West is easier to say. So English people began calling the island Key West."

I wished I had seen the island of bones. But . . . too late for that now. I studied the passengers. Nobody looked like a kidnapper.

I hated wasting all this time. So I studied people on the street. No kidnapper types there either.

We passed the oldest house in Key West. It was very small. We passed a man selling shells.

The guide told us about Audubon House. Audubon was famous for studying and painting birds. He visited the Florida Keys in 1832.

We stopped at Hemingway House. Hemingway was a famous author who liked six-toed cats.

When we drove on, I noticed something. The boy who wouldn't sit beside me was gone. I looked all around. But he was really gone. Maybe he got off to pet the six-toed cats.

At last the tour ended, and we walked home. Mom fixed us lunch. She reminded us of the directions to day camp. Then she left for work.

We walked slowly, and I watched for kidnappers. No, not the fat lady. She didn't match Angela's description. For a while, I watched a man. But he seemed too short. Angela had said a *tall* man. Then I nudged Maria.

"There," I said. I nodded and pointed. This man towered over everyone. Stilts. I nicknamed him quickly.

He looked suspicious to me. He wore a black sweatband on his forehead. He wore cutoff jeans and a tank top.

He carried a small notebook and a pen. He headed down an alley. What sort of guys walked down alleys?

"Let's follow him," I said. "Maybe he's looking for his next victim."

"What happened to caution?" Maria asked. "Your mom said . . ."

"We'll be careful," I said. "He won't notice us."

Maria held back. "No," she said. "Don't go there. Your mom said . . ."

THE CASE OF THE DISAPPEARING KIDNAPPER

Bossy Maria! I didn't let her finish. The guy looked like a kidnapper to me. I turned down the alley, pulling Maria along.

We kept a safe distance behind Stilts. He stopped and turned the page in his notebook. Probably spotting kids to kidnap later, I thought.

He peered at something on the side of the house. Then he walked on. We walked on too. Stilts stopped at every house. He wrote in his notebook every time he stopped. Must be lots of kids living along here, I thought.

Wow! Wait until we told a policeman about this guy! We might get our pictures in the paper again. I might really be on my way to being an eponym. *He's a regular Cody Smith.* I could hear the police saying it now.

Then Stilts turned down another alley. It was filled with tangled weeds and vines.

"I'm going back," Maria said. "This place scares me. I'm staying on the route to day camp."

Drat Maria! The man heard her. Now he turned to face us. At first he looked surprised to see us. Then his eyes looked dark and mean.

He walked toward us. I wanted to run, but I couldn't. Fear nailed me right to the spot.

5

Stranger on the Prowl

Stilts came closer and closer. But I still couldn't move. Neither could Maria. His heels scraped against the bricked alley.

I could taste copper on the back of my tongue. It was as if I had a penny in my mouth. I know that's the taste of fear.

Caution is a good thing in a detective. Mom's voice replayed in my mind. But it was too late.

"Why are you kids following me?" Stilts asked. His angry voice rumbled like a kettle drum. That's how I thought a kidnapper's voice would sound.

Maria spoke up. Sometimes she can make a tense situation better.

"We were walking to Sea View Park," Maria said. "And . . ."

Stilts scowled. But he kept his distance.

"Maybe we sort of lost our way," I said.

"Maybe," Stilts agreed. "Or maybe you're just nosy kids."

Now he smiled. Surely kidnappers didn't spend much time smiling. My mouth felt dry. But the coppery taste left it.

"It's okay, kids," Stilts said. "Sometimes curiosity can be a good thing. But I'm no burglar, if that's what you think. I work for the city."

"Doing what?" I asked. I hadn't thought about him being a burglar.

Maybe I couldn't be an eponym right off. Maybe I'd have to work up to it. First burglars. Then kidnappers. And maybe some stuff in between.

"I'm reading electric meters," Stilts said. "It's an alley sort of job. There's a meter on the back of each house."

Now I saw the meters. I felt stupid. Detectives needed to notice details like electric meters.

"You two head back toward the street," Stilts said. "Turn right. You'll find the park."

"Thank you, mister," Maria said.

We turned and ran. I looked back once. Was Stilts following us? No. He stood reading the next meter.

We paused on a corner to catch our breath. Maria didn't mention Stilts. I didn't either. After a few minutes, we walked on to the day camp.

Hibiscus bushes circled Sea View Park. Kids sat at palm-shaded tables. I noticed a bald man driving by in an old Ford.

I probably wouldn't have noticed him. But he drove around the block twice. He stared right at us. Then he pretended to be looking at the trees.

The kidnapper? The thought hung in my mind, but Baldy drove on. I didn't mention my suspicions to Maria.

We soon saw the camp director. She was tall. And she was a redhead. I liked that about her. She wore a paint-smudged jumpsuit with a long necklace made of seashells.

She said to call her Shelly. The name suited her. We told her Rosa Sanchez had sent us. She smiled.

"My name's Cody Smith," I said. Shelly laughed. I hate it when people laugh at my name. I told her so.

"I'm not laughing at your name," Shelly said. "I laughed because Smith's my name too. It's a common name."

"I'll tell you a secret," I said. "Long ago, everyone was named Smith." I saw Maria back away. She'd heard my story many times before. But I told it to Shelly.

"When a Smith did something wrong, the rest of the Smiths punished him. They made him change his name. These days, there are hardly any of us Smiths left."

Shelly smiled. "I'll save that tale for anyone who laughs at *my* name," she said.

Shelly introduced us to the campers. Then I spotted the boy. It was the same boy who ignored me on the Conch Train. I was surprised.

Now he motioned me to sit by him. And I did. Maybe I'd learn why he snubbed me. Maria sat beside some girls at another table.

"My name's Bob Deed," the boy said. "And I heard your name—Cody Smith."

Bob wore cool green biking shorts and a silvery tank top. I saw a large shiny ring on his left thumb. I felt dorky in my cutoffs and polo shirt.

Suddenly I felt chilly. On this hot day, a cool breeze rustled the palm fronds.

"Bob," Shelly said, "please share your craft supplies with Cody. Okay?"

"Sure, Shelly." Bob shoved the supplies between us. "You can have them all. Today I'm writing in my journal."

I sighed. Maybe Bob should sit by Maria. They could talk about journals.

"What are you writing about?" I asked him.

"I'm writing about Key West," Bob said. "My friends in Nrutas want to know what it's like."

"Nrutas?" I asked. "Where's that? Is it in Florida?"

"No," Bob said. "It's far away." Bob shoved a pattern and a ruler toward me. "The others are making kites. You'll need to figure how much paper you'll need."

Kites! What fun! I studied the pattern and started measuring.

"Want some help?" Bob asked.

"Sure. I'd hate to make a big mistake on my first day."

Bob glanced at my pattern. "You'll need a piece a yard square," he said.

I felt another whiff of cool air. "How do you know?" I asked. "You didn't add any numbers."

"I just know." Bob began writing in his notebook.

When Shelly checked my work, she smiled. "Exactly right, Cody. Choose any color paper you like. Mark the cutting lines. I'll check them before you cut."

I chose blue paper and began measuring. I looked up. I sensed that Bob was watching.

What an eerie feeling! Bob pretended he hadn't been watching. I wanted to let him know I'd caught him.

But I saw Baldy in the old Ford again. I felt like a shark spotting its prey. I walked over to Maria. She stopped working on her kite and listened.

"Maybe Baldy's the kidnapper, Maria," I whispered. "Sea View Park would be a good place to find a kid."

"Tell Shelly," Maria said. "That's what you should do. Tell her right now."

Bossy Maria! I shook my head. "She might scare him off."

"You just want to be the one to turn him in," Maria said. "Big deal."

Sometimes Maria saw through my schemes. But then Baldy drove away. So I didn't have to decide what to do.

Maria's notebook lay open on the table. I peeked at it.

Only one person in a billion will live to be 116.

I didn't believe it. She made that stuff up. I knew it!

By late afternoon we finished our kites. No time to

fly them today. I turned to tell Bob good-bye. But he had already left.

I had forgotten about Baldy until we started home. There! I saw him again. Now he was walking slowly around the park. Where was his Ford?

I think he saw us. But he looked up into the trees.

"Let's follow him," I said to Maria. "I think he might be the kidnapper."

"No way!" Maria said. "Didn't you learn anything from following that meter reader?"

Okay. Bossy Maria was right. I was about to admit it. But she went on talking. She did that sometimes.

"What if he *is* the kidnapper?" Maria said. "Then what? I'm going straight home. That's what we promised to do."

"Tell you what, Maria," I said. "We'll find a police officer. He'll help us catch Baldy. That should be safe enough."

And that's what we did. A motorcycle cop rode toward us. I stepped into the street and stopped him.

He wore dark pants, a white shirt, and a helmet. He had one blue eye and one brown eye. Interesting. I couldn't think of a nickname to fit that.

I explained about Baldy watching the day camp.

"He could be a kidnapper, officer," I said. "He's over on the other side of the park."

"So let's go talk to him," the policeman said. Maria grabbed my wrist as we headed toward the kidnapper.

6

The Secret Ring

Suddenly the policeman smiled. Smiling at a kidnapper? I could hardly believe it.

Baldy saw us coming, but he didn't run. Another surprise.

Baldy and the officer shook hands. What was going on here? I was about to run, but the officer's words stopped me.

"Kids, meet Mr. Hankins. And Mr. Hankins, meet Cody and Maria. They've noticed you driving around the park. They're curious."

Mr. Hankins shook our hands. Then he smiled. "I've been waiting for your day camp to end. I needed to get inside the park. I'm a county tree inspector."

I didn't tell him we thought he was a kidnapper. "Why are you inspecting trees?" I asked.

"Several reasons," Mr. Hankins said. "Trees are precious in the Keys. They need care and attention. They need protection from abuse."

"I thought trees just sort of grew without any help," Maria said.

"Sometimes they do," Mr. Hankins said. "But at times, palm trees become diseased. If we catch the disease quickly, we may cure it. I look for withered fronds."

"Did you see any here?" I asked. The fronds all looked green enough to me.

"No," Mr. Hankins said. "These palms look healthy. I also inspect for tree abuse. Sometimes people nail their clotheslines to a tree. Or they may tie an electrical cord to a branch. Those acts can damage trees. I issue warnings."

Maria gave me an "I-told-you-so" look. I hated being wrong twice in the same day. Was I ever glad the policeman didn't mention our suspicions! We said good-bye to Baldy and walked away.

"Thank you, officer," I said. "I'm sorry we bothered you."

"No problem," he said. "Whenever you suspect trouble, go to a police officer. That's what we're here for."

Maria and I headed for Blossom Street. Maria walked about two steps ahead. Mom said the person walking ahead is usually the one who's mad. Right, Mom. Maria was like a wasp in a bottle.

"That's it, Cody!" Maria said. She panted because we were walking so fast. "I'm not helping you find the kidnapper. Forget it before you land in big trouble."

I didn't answer. A page slipped from her journal, and I picked it up.

> **When ketchup leaves the bottle, it travels at a rate of 25 miles per year.**

I didn't laugh. I just returned the page. She didn't say thanks. When we reached home, Mom broke the tension.

"Surprise," she called. She pointed to the open car trunk. "Bicycles. One for each of us. I rented them in town."

"Neat," I shouted. Maria and I helped lift them from the trunk. We had both ridden bikes in Central Park in New York.

"May I have the red one?" Maria asked.

I really wanted that one. But I let Maria have it. I didn't want any more arguments with her today.

"We'll leave the car in the driveway," Mom said. "It's easier to get around these narrow streets on a bicycle."

Maria and I rode around the block. We waved at Gypsy and Angela. Then we went inside for supper.

Mom cooked again. I think she's tired of grilled cheese sandwiches. She made spaghetti and garlic toast. Yummy!

After supper we rode clear around the island. Neat! We stopped and rested at the beach.

People were still swimming. Others were flying kites. Farther from shore, speedboats pulled water-skiers.

"Maybe sometime I'll try that," I said.

Mom rolled her eyes. So did Maria.

The next day we rode our bikes to day camp. Bob beat us there. He'd saved me a place.

Today was storytelling day. All of us told a story about our home or our family. Everyone but Bob. He smiled and shook his head. Maria told about hunting Bigfoot in Central Park. I told about the tornado at Gram's house.

And then it was lunchtime. I had made us peanut butter sandwiches. Maria ate with the girls. I followed Bob to a shady patch of grass under a palm tree.

"Why wouldn't you tell about your home?" I asked.

Bob shrugged. "I'm just here for a short time."

"Do you have any other friends in Key West?" I asked.

"No," Bob said.

I wasn't surprised. Bob snubbed people. And they snubbed him back. That was a rotten way to make friends.

"Well, I'll be your friend," I said. "Want to ride my bike?"

"Maybe sometime," Bob said.

"Maybe you'd like to come home with me some afternoon," I said. "We have a neat old house."

"I'd like that," Bob said. "You're the first person who's invited me to do anything."

"I'll ask Mom about having you over," I promised. "Maybe tomorrow."

We ate in silence for a while. Then Bob pulled the ring from his thumb.

"Hey," I said. "That's *three* rings, isn't it? I thought it was just one big one."

Bob held one of the rings toward me. "Want to wear it? It's a secret friendship ring. If you wear it, we'll be friends forever. It's a good luck ring too."

I hesitated. I hardly knew Bob. How did I know I'd want to be his friend forever? But I hated to hurt his feelings. I could return the ring if friendship forever didn't work out.

"Sure," I said. "It's really neat."

The ring from Bob's thumb fit my middle finger. It was strange that it felt cold on such a hot day.

That afternoon Shelly read us a mystery story. After that, we listened to music. Then it was dismissal time.

"Walk a ways with me?" Bob invited. "I'll take you to Dog Beach."

"How about it?" I asked Maria to join us. I hoped she wouldn't notice my new ring. She might think it was weird that Bob had given me a friendship ring.

"Okay," Maria said. "But we shouldn't stay long."

"Can I get on the bike with you?" Bob asked me.

"No," I said. "That's against the law. I'll push the bike and we'll walk."

We walked a long way to Dog Beach. But I didn't complain. I was glad Maria didn't complain either. Friends don't like friends who whine. At last we arrived at a tiny beach.

"It's the only beach where people can bring dogs," Bob explained.

THE CASE OF THE DISAPPEARING KIDNAPPER

One look at the sand and I knew why. Maria and I stepped carefully as we followed Bob.

Bob climbed up on a slippery seawall. He stretched a hand to help me up. And I helped Maria.

To our left, the tide surged onto the sand. But below the seawall, the bottom dropped off into deep water. The sea splashed against the concrete wall. I felt it dampen my legs and shoes. I even tasted salt on my lips.

I shaded my eyes from the sun. A cargo ship was far out to sea. Closer to shore, three shrimpers lay at anchor. Bob knew they were shrimpers from their trawling nets. Nearby, three sailboats caught the afternoon breeze.

I felt uneasy on the seawall. I turned to jump down. But suddenly I lost my balance and fell backward. I hit the water with a big splash. Then the sea closed over my head.

7

The Weird Notebook

I struggled to the surface. I was choking and gasping for air. Saltwater stung my eyes. I felt like I'd inhaled fiery balloons. I hated that feeling inside my lungs.

"Cody!" Maria shouted.

Was I ever glad to hear her voice! The tide banged me against the seawall. Barnacles scraped my shoulder.

I saw Maria's outstretched hand. I clutched at it. She pulled me from the deep water onto the seawall.

"What a fall!" Maria exclaimed. "Did seeing all that swirling water make you dizzy?"

"I didn't fall," I said. "Someone pushed me." I glared at Maria. Then I looked around for Bob. Maria and I were alone.

"Well, I didn't push you," Maria said. "Where did Bob go? Do you think he shoved you?"

I coughed and spluttered again. I needed time to think about this. Maybe I *had* fallen.

I felt my friendship ring. Bob said we'd be friends forever. He wouldn't have pushed me. I looked back at Maria.

"Maria, if you pushed me . . ."

"Cody! I didn't push you," Maria stated.

I looked her in the eye. "I think you're just a little jealous of Bob."

"Why would I be jealous of him?" Maria asked.

"Maybe because he wants to be my friend," I said. "Maybe you feel left out."

"No way," Maria said. She drew an *X* over her heart with her forefinger. "Cross my heart. I didn't push you. And I think Bob's weird. He has a strange look in his eyes."

"Maybe I just got clumsy," I said. I believed Maria. She doesn't do mean things.

I felt my friendship ring again. Would Bob have pushed me? "Did you see Bob leave?"

"No," Maria said. "Maybe your fall scared him. Maybe he ran for help."

"Look!" I cried. "There's his notebook. There behind that clump of sea oats."

I ran to the notebook and picked it up. When I started to open it, Maria stopped me.

"Maybe it's private," Maria said. "I wouldn't want anyone opening my journal."

"Bob's notebook is different," I said. "He told me about it. He's writing descriptions of Key West. They're for his friends back home. They want to know about Key West."

"Where's his home?" Maria asked.

"Nrutas," I said. "I don't know where that is. But Bob said it's far away from here. It's not in Florida."

I opened the notebook and stared. What strange writing! I turned the notebook upside down. I turned it sideways.

"This is weird, Maria," I said. "There aren't any words. The pages are full of squiggles. And squares. Well, they're not quite squares either."

"And look at those triangle shapes," Maria said. "They're not quite true triangles. Your friend Bob is weird. Know what I think?"

"What?" I asked.

"Maybe he can't read," Maria said. "Some kids have trouble reading. Maybe he tries to cover it up by writing squiggles. Or maybe he's an orphan from Kosovo. Maybe this is how people from Kosovo write."

"No," I said. "I think they use letters just like we do. I'll take his book to him tomorrow. And I won't tell him we peeked."

I felt really sorry for anyone who couldn't read. They missed so much fun.

My clothes dried out by the time we reached home. But the saltwater made my skin itch. I took a quick shower before Mom arrived.

"Let's not tell her I fell into the water," I said. "It would worry her. She might say we can't bike to the beach."

I rubbed Bob's friendship ring. Bob had said it would bring luck. So far I hadn't seen any of that luck.

"Right," Maria agreed. "We won't tell. I know it won't happen again."

I was about to step onto the front porch. Then I saw a man on the sidewalk. He stood staring at Angela's house.

I made quick mental notes in my brain. That's what detectives do sometimes. Short. Pudgy. Khaki jumpsuit. Wide-brimmed straw hat that hid his face.

"What do you suppose that guy's doing?" I whispered. He couldn't hear me. But something about him made me want to whisper. "I don't like his looks. I think he's hiding under that hat."

"Maybe he's the kidnapper," Maria said. "Maybe he's after Angela again. Let's call her mother and warn her."

"Good idea," I said. I found the number in the phone book. Maria dialed. But nobody answered.

"Guess Angela's safe as long as she's not home," Maria said.

"He's got a clipboard," I said. "Maybe he's casing the house. What if he returns later? He'll know right where all the windows and doors are."

"Should we call the police?" Maria asked.

"Mom says never to call the police," I said, "unless you're sure it's really necessary. And we aren't really sure."

"We could call Mrs. Sanchez," Maria said. "She might even know the guy. Maybe he's just another meter reader or something."

I dialed and Gypsy answered quickly. I whispered our problem. She said she couldn't hear me. So I talked loud.

"You kids stay inside," she said. "I'll come right over. We'll see what's going on. I don't like strangers prowling around the neighborhood."

I watched Gypsy walk boldly across the street. Her bracelets jangled. The man went on writing on his clipboard. He didn't even look up.

Maybe he was used to jangling bracelets. Or maybe he didn't hear well. Gypsy stepped into our living room.

"Do you know that man?" I asked Gypsy.

"No," she said. "I don't like him nosing around so close to my house. But I'm not afraid of him." She drew herself up to her full height. I guessed she was a foot taller than Straw Hat.

"You're not going out there, are you?" Maria asked.

"That's exactly what I'm going to do," Gypsy said. "He's not big enough to kidnap *me*."

"We're coming with you," I said. I looked at Maria, hoping she'd back me up.

"Yeah," Maria said. "We're coming with you."

I thought Maria's voice sounded feeble. But she followed Gypsy and me outside.

Just then I saw Mom pedaling toward us. She had on her black wig and her scary eyebrows. And she was wearing her long dress. Now there would be four of us to confront Straw Hat.

"What's going on here?" Mom asked.

I wanted to shush her, but it was too late. Straw Hat had turned to look at us. And now he began walking right toward us.

His hat still hid his eyes. When he put one hand in his pocket, I wanted to run. But Gypsy called to him in a strong voice.

"Good afternoon, sir," Gypsy said. "The Gomez family is away right now. We're neighbors. Is there something we can do to help you?"

8

A Glow in the Dark

Straw Hat walked toward us. I rubbed my good luck ring. We needed all the luck we could get.

Straw Hat pushed his hat back so we could see his eyes. Then he smiled and shook hands with Gypsy.

Now he didn't seem scary at all. In a way, I felt glad. I didn't like the idea of a kidnapper in the neighborhood. In another way, I felt sad. I'd lost another chance to be an eponym.

I thought about Mr. Leotard. He was a French trapeze artist. Dancers still call their outfits *leotards*.

And I thought about R. J. Guppy. He discovered a new fish. Scientists named it after him.

I grabbed a deep breath and prepared to face Straw Hat. I couldn't give up my goal now.

"My name's George Adbury," Straw Hat said. "I work for the Key West Tourist Bureau. We're planning a walking tour for visitors."

"On Blossom Street?" Gypsy asked.

"Oh my, yes," Straw Hat said. "There are several historic houses here. The Gomez house, for example. It's quite special."

We all looked at Angela's purple house. It didn't seem so special to me. Except for being purple. It reminded me of a grape lollipop.

"It's called an Eyebrow House," Straw Hat said. "Look at those four windows under the roof overhang. Don't they remind you of eyebrows?"

They didn't remind me of eyebrows. But I kept quiet. This was starting to be a boring conversation.

"And the house has no nails in it," Straw Hat said.

That caught my attention. "So what holds it together?" I asked.

"Tongue-and-groove joints," Straw Hat said. "They're fastened with wooden pegs. This house was built in the Bahama Islands. Carpenters tore it apart. Then they shipped it to Key West and fitted it together again. We want this house on our walking tour."

Straw Hat mentioned other things too. He talked about hand-carved trim. And roof hatches. I knew about roof hatches. Our house had those. He said they helped keep houses cool. I liked air-conditioning better. But I didn't say that.

Straw Hat talked for a long time. Then he said good-bye and walked on to another house. Mom thanked Gypsy for helping us. Then we went inside.

"What's that notebook you're carrying?" Mom asked.

I thought fast. "It belongs to a friend I met at day camp," I said. "His name's Bob Deed. He went off without the notebook this afternoon. So I picked it up for him. Guess he forgot it."

"Where does he live?" Mom asked. "Maybe we should return it to him. Or call him to say you've found it. He's probably missed it. And he's probably worried."

"I don't know where he lives," I said. "I just see him at the park."

"Maybe his name and address are inside the notebook," Mom said. She opened the notebook and looked at the strange pictures. "Is he an artist?"

"I don't know," I said. "But he spends lots of time drawing this stuff."

We looked in the telephone book. But we didn't find any Deed name listed.

"We could call Shelly Smith," Maria said. "She's the camp director. She would have Bob's address. She told me she lives on Union Street."

"Look up her number, please," Mom said. "This disguise is hot. I need to change into something cooler."

Mom went upstairs. Good. I liked to see her in mother clothes instead of disguises.

Maria and I looked for Shelly's phone number. There were lots of Smiths in Key West. Three of them lived on Union Street. It took time, but we found Shelly's number.

We waited until Mom came downstairs. We let her do the calling.

When she finished, she had Bob's phone number. And his address on Ocean Vista Street. She wrote it down—1505 Ocean Vista.

"Why don't you call him?" Mom asked me. "He's your friend."

I dialed the number. A recorded voice delivered a message. "The number you're dialing can't be reached." Sometimes I make dialing mistakes. So I tried again. I got the same recording.

"Why don't we ride our bikes to his house?" Mom

asked. "We all need the exercise. And I'd like to meet Bob."

That didn't surprise me. It was Mom's habit to know who my friends are. I liked that habit. I liked knowing that one parent still cared about me.

I was curious about Bob too. I wanted to see where he lived. I wanted to see what his folks were like.

"It's awfully hot," Maria said.

"So let's eat supper first," Mom said. "It'll be cooler a little later. I've bought avocados. Cody, you get out the bread. And pour the iced tea. I'll peel the avocados for sandwiches. Maria, you make a fruit salad."

And that was what we did. I hadn't tasted avocados before. They felt slick on my tongue. Like boiled asparagus. I didn't like that feeling so much. But they tasted bland and good. A change from grilled cheese.

We cleaned up the kitchen. Then we found a Key West map in the phone book.

Ocean Vista Street was a long way off. There were lots of turns to remember. I wrote them all down. Mom said finding Bob's home would be easy.

We stopped to tell Gypsy where we were going. Mom always lets someone know where she'll be. She says that's a good idea. Even for adults.

Maria put on her headphones. She turned on her radio. We traveled about a mile to our first turn. We rode single file.

Traffic whizzed past us. Cars were heading for sunset at Mallory Dock. At Simonton Street, we turned left. Edward Street was narrow and winding. It was bumpy too. Now there were fewer cars.

At the end of Edward Street, we reached a T intersection.

"Let's turn right," Mom said. "Watch the house numbers. We're in the 700 block here. The numbers should get larger."

"But they don't, Mom." I said. "They're getting smaller."

So we turned around and headed the other way. Now the street numbers grew larger. Soon we were in the 900s. Larger. Larger.

"Here's the 1500 block," Maria said. She had taken her headphones off. Now she pointed to a street sign on the corner.

Here the house numbers were harder to see. Sometimes vines grew over them. Sometimes the houses had no numbers. Finally we reached the last house on Ocean Vista. A man and woman sat on the porch of number 1503.

"There must be a mistake," Mom said. "There isn't any 1505."

"You're sure Shelly said 1505?" I asked.

"I'm sure," Mom said. "I don't like this at all. It's nearly dusk. We need to be heading home."

THE CASE OF THE DISAPPEARING KIDNAPPER

I agreed with Mom. This street was spooky. Bob could wait until tomorrow to get his notebook back. But just then the man stepped from the porch.

"May I help you folks?" he asked.

"Thank you, sir," Mom said. "We're hunting for the Deed residence. The number is 1505."

The man shook his head. "Maybe you have the wrong street name," he said. "Our house is the last one on Ocean Vista."

"Do you know the Deed family?" Mom asked.

Again the man shook his head. "No, ma'am. No Deed family around here. We've lived here for many years. Never heard of the Deeds."

Mom thanked the man. We headed home. I didn't admit to Mom and Maria that I was scared. But I rubbed my good luck ring.

It glowed in the dark! Weird! Bob hadn't mentioned that it glowed in the dark.

Suddenly I sensed someone watching us. My scalp tingled. I looked around. But no one was there.

9

A Time of Surprises

Nobody said much until we got home. We were tired. And disappointed.

I guess nobody had been watching me after all. My scalp stopped tingling.

"Cody," Mom said, "I want to meet your friend Bob."

"Sure, Mom," I said. "Want to visit camp tomorrow?"

"I have to work," Mom said. "Why not invite Bob here? We'll have pizza for supper. He should like that."

"Sure, Mom. I'll ask him tomorrow. I think he'll come. He's a loner. I think he needs some friends."

Once in bed, I couldn't sleep. I kept remembering my fall from the seawall. Yes. It had been a fall. Bob had no reason to push me. But all night I dreamed about water closing over my head.

The next morning, Maria yelled at me. "Come on, slowpoke. Let's not be late for camp."

Bossy Maria! We walked to the park. I tucked Bob's notebook under my shirt. We were the first ones there. But Bob arrived soon.

He wore the same green biking shorts. The same silvery T-shirt. And they still looked clean. Florida's really hot. Nobody wears the same clothes a bunch of times.

I thought Bob looked surprised to see me. Had he pushed me? Did he think I had drowned?

"We looked for your house yesterday," Maria said. "There was no house at 1505 Ocean Vista."

"You had the wrong street," Bob said. "It's Sea Vista, not Ocean Vista."

I didn't believe that. Shelly had said Ocean Vista. But I didn't argue. I returned Bob's notebook. "You left it yesterday at Dog Beach."

"Thanks," Bob said.

That's all he said. Just "thanks." No explanation about his strange writing. No apology for ditching us. That made me mad.

But Mom wanted to meet him. So I'd invite him. I felt my friendship ring. Neat. Yeah, we were friends. Maybe.

"How about coming home with us today?" I asked. "Mom says it's okay. We're having pizza for supper."

"I'd really like that," Bob said. He leaned forward. He smiled and his eyes sparkled.

He seemed eager to come. I liked that. Yet he puzzled me. Didn't he have to ask his mother first? That worried me. I didn't want to get in trouble with his mom.

Maybe Maria was right. Maybe Bob was a homeless person. That would explain the bad address. And not needing permission.

But it didn't explain his clean clothes. Moms are usually the ones who keep clothes clean. Bob was like a puzzle with several missing pieces.

Our camp day passed quickly. Shelly led a hike to the beach. I looked for shells. But I didn't find any. Shelly said there was a coral reef offshore. It kept most shells from washing onto the beach.

Bob and I built a sandcastle. Then Bob looked into the distance.

"Hey," he said. "I see a shell. Let's go get it."

He left the group. I went along, but Shelly called us back. We returned to the park. It was time to go home. Bob walked with us.

Maria offered us cinnamon balls. I declined, but Bob took one. He unwrapped the candy and popped it into his mouth. He rolled the candy around on his tongue, exploring its shape and taste.

"This is good," he said, sounding surprised. "Thank you."

"You're welcome. Want to try my headphones?" Maria asked.

Maria put her radio in Bob's shirt pocket. She slipped the headphones over his ears. Bob jumped. His eyes grew wide. What was he hearing?

I lifted one earphone. I heard someone singing rap. What was so surprising about that?

Once at home, we began making pizza. Maria used a tube of biscuits. She rolled the dough into a ball. Then she flattened it on the pizza pan.

I opened the can of sauce. I let Bob spread it on the dough. Mom would add other stuff when she got home.

I didn't say anything when Bob dropped the spoon. Then he almost spilled the sauce. What a klutz!

"Your first time in the kitchen?" Maria asked.

"Yes," Bob said. Maria rolled her eyes.

Then Mom came in. She wore her orange pot-scrubber wig. She had on a long green dress with six necklaces. Bob really looked surprised when she pulled off her phony nose and her wig.

"Mom's a detective," I explained. "She wears disguises at work."

"Oh," Bob said.

"Maybe Bob would like to see our house," Mom said. "Ever seen a widow's walk, Bob?"

"No," Bob said. "You have a widow here?"

Mom explained about the widow's walk. "Take him up the ladder," Mom said. "Show him the view."

So we walked upstairs. We stepped onto the second-story porch for a moment. Then Bob leaned over the railing to look downstairs. Maria yanked on his shirttail before he fell over. I pulled him toward the ladder in my closet.

Maria began climbing first. She opened the trapdoor.

I went up second. When I reached the widow's walk, I turned around. I thought Bob was right behind me. But he wasn't.

"Bob," I called to him. "Bob, come on up."

No answer. We both called again. "Bob! Bob!"

"Maybe he went back to the porch," Maria said.

We ran downstairs. No Bob. Mom helped us search. Still no Bob.

I looked into the banyan. Maybe Bob liked to climb trees. Sun glinting on a silvery airplane blinded me. A few seconds passed before I could see again. But Bob hadn't climbed the banyan.

"What could have happened to him?" Maria asked. "Maybe it's time to call the police. Maybe he's been kidnapped!"

"Let's look around again," Mom said. "Surely Bob's here somewhere."

We looked upstairs. We looked downstairs. We looked in the yard. No Bob. Mom picked up the telephone. Just then Bob walked into the kitchen.

"Bob, where have you been?" Mom asked. "We looked everywhere for you. Didn't you hear us calling?"

Bob stood very straight. He looked at a spot just above Mom's head. He wouldn't look her in the eye.

"I went back onto the second-floor porch," he said. "I'd seen a tiny lizard. I leaned over the railing to see it again. And I fell."

"Oh, my goodness!" Mom exclaimed. "Are you all right? Did you hurt yourself?" She looked Bob over carefully. "Maybe you hit your head. You must have knocked yourself out. Didn't you hear us calling you?"

"No," Bob said. "I didn't hear you. But I landed in some bushes. I'm not hurt. I'm sorry I frightened you."

I looked at Bob. Then I looked at Maria. And she looked at me. Neither of us believed Bob's story.

We had circled the house. He hadn't been there. It surprised me that Mom seemed to believe Bob's tale. Surely she was a better detective than that!

Bob's clothes weren't mussed up. No dirt clung to his face or hands. And he seemed very calm.

That's not how most kids would act. Not if they'd fallen off a high place. But Bob convinced Mom he felt okay.

We all washed up for supper. Mom had put the finishing touches on the pizza. It looked perfect—lots of cheese and hamburger and olives and mushrooms. Wow!

We let Bob have the first piece. I thought he'd take a big bite right away. But he just held it and looked at it. I had a feeling that he'd never eaten pizza before. Maybe they didn't have pizza in Nrutas.

I couldn't wait any longer. I took a big bite. And so did Mom and Maria.

Bob began eating then too. And he liked it. He ate four pieces. After supper, he helped us do the dishes.

"Will you two come home with me tomorrow?" Bob asked. "We can have fun at my house too."

"I'd like that, Bob," I said. "What can we do at your house?"

"Oh, it's near the beach," Bob said. "We can fly kites."

"Okay," I said. "That sounds cool."

Maria went upstairs to write in her journal. Bob and I rode the bicycles around the block.

"Cody," Mom called. "It'll be dark soon. It's time to take Bob home."

"No thank you, Mrs. Smith," Bob said. "I'll walk home. I like to walk."

I knew Mom wanted to see where Bob lived. But she was too late. Bob dropped his bike. He headed home before we could stop him.

Walking? No way. He ran. He hadn't thanked us for the supper. He hadn't even said he had a good time.

10

Nrutas

We talked about Bob for a long time after he left. Maria didn't like him. Mom didn't know what to think of him. Neither did I.

69

The next morning, Maria glared at me.

"Cody," she said. "I'm not going to Bob's house today. He's weird. I don't trust him."

"Well, I'm going," I said. "He's such a loner. I feel sorry for him." I rubbed my friendship ring.

"Kids," Mom said. "Bob's mother may not be expecting either of you."

"Yeah," Maria said. "He didn't call to ask permission."

"We still don't know where he lives," Mom said. "You two walk to camp today. Maria, come on home after camp if you want to. Cody, I'll pick you and Bob up afterward. We'll drive to Bob's house. I may be a little late. So wait for me at the park."

"Okay," I said. "Will do."

Maria said nothing. She was writing in her journal. I peeked again.

> The world's termites outweigh the world's humans ten to one.

So who cares? I wondered. Where does she get those crazy facts? What if her facts are wrong? Are they still called facts?

Today a magician visited day camp. He said he performed each night at Mallory Dock. He did lots of tricks.

But he wouldn't show us how he did them. He said that magicians never tell. But afterward, Bob did lots of the same tricks.

Bob found a quarter in my ear. He made a button disappear. And he pulled a banana from Maria's sleeve.

"How'd you learn to do that?" I asked.

"I just watched the magician," Bob said.

Very strange, I thought. Maria and I couldn't do any of the tricks. And we had watched the magician too. Bob just shrugged and laughed.

In the afternoon, Shelly taught us sea chanteys. They're long-ago sailor songs. And pirate songs. Lots of yo-ho-ho stuff. We liked them a lot.

Maria headed home when camp ended. She hadn't changed her mind about Bob. Bob and I waited for Mom.

"You boys okay?" Shelly asked.

"Yes," I said. "Mom's coming for us in the car. We're to wait right here for her."

"All right," Shelly said. "I'll see you tomorrow." She rode off on her motorbike.

"Your mother's late," Bob said. "Let's walk on home."

"No," I said. "I promised her I'd wait. Let's stand here on the corner. She'll be here soon."

"I hate waiting," Bob said. "Come on. We don't need a ride. It's just a short walk."

"I'm waiting," I said. I watched the other kids walking home. Some were already over a block away.

Others still hung around an ice cream stand. That's it, I thought, stalling for time. Ice cream.

"Bob," I said. "I'll treat. Let's have a cone."

"A cone?" Bob asked.

"Sure," I said. Hadn't he ever eaten a cone? "How about chocolate?"

I ran to the ice cream stand. I bought two chocolate cones before Bob could argue. They began melting immediately.

Chocolate stained my shirt. But Bob didn't drip a drop. Some neatnik! How'd he manage that?

"Cody," Bob said. "Let's go. Your mom has forgotten you. Maybe she's out chasing a crook."

"Mom keeps her promises," I said. But I began to believe Bob was right. Mom had forgotten.

"Let's start walking," Bob said. "Maybe she'll see us and stop."

Bob looked directly at me. Something in his gaze told me he was right. Mom would see us. She would stop.

I walked along with Bob. Why not see where he lived?

"How far to your house?" I asked.

"Not far," Bob said. "Are you still wearing my ring?"

I held up my hand so he could see the ring. He surprised me. He removed another section of his own ring. He slipped it on my finger too. It stuck to the first ring. They became one.

"Now we are double friends," Bob said.

"What are double friends?" I asked. But Bob didn't answer. He just smiled.

We walked on. What if Mom couldn't see us? What if she didn't find me? I'd be in big-time trouble.

"How much farther?" I asked.

"Just a little way," Bob said. He grabbed my wrist. He walked faster, pulling me along.

We had reached the beach. It was the deserted part. I really didn't want to go there. But somehow I couldn't say no to Bob.

Then I saw a strange thing in the sky. It looked like a huge silver football. Sun glinting on it hurt my eyes.

"Bob!" I cried. "What is that thing?"

Did Bob answer? I'm not sure. The wind started to blow. And the world began to spin. I had never felt so dizzy.

But just then Mom arrived in the car. She jumped out and called my name.

Bob held my wrist tightly. I couldn't break away, and sand blew into my eyes. I couldn't see. I felt Mom yanking on my other hand.

"Come on, Bob," I shouted. "Let's ride with Mom."

Suddenly my arm fell limp at my side. The wind stopped blowing. I couldn't see Bob. Mom pulled me to our car and opened the door.

"Why are you on this deserted beach?" she asked. "And that sudden windstorm! It's a wonder I ever found you."

"You didn't come for us," I said. "Bob and I decided to walk on. Where were you?"

"I had a flat tire," Mom said. "I came as soon as I could. But don't tell tall tales. Bob's not with you. There's nobody else here. Nobody at all."

I looked all around. Mom was right. Where had Bob gone? And the big silver football was gone too.

I didn't even try to tell Mom about that. I wasn't sure I'd seen it myself. Maybe I'd imagined it.

"Mom," I said. "Bob and I thought you'd see us. He was with me a minute ago."

"What is Bob's last name?" Mom asked. "I'm going to talk to Shelly about him. Tomorrow I'll visit your day camp."

"His name's Bob Deed," I said. "Don't get him in trouble, Mom. I like him a lot."

"Well, I'm glad you're okay," Mom said. "But I *will* talk to Shelly. I want to know more about your new friend."

Mom relaxed as we drove toward home. "Bob Deed," she said. "Strange names."

"What's so strange about them?" I asked.

Mom shrugged. "Both names spell the same forward or backward. Weird!"

I wrote the names out. Sure enough. Mom was right. Palindromes. We'd studied words like that at school.

Mom didn't say any more about Bob. And I didn't tell Maria all of what had happened. She might laugh. She might write it down with the other weird stuff in her journal.

That night Mom locked the house very carefully. We went to bed.

I never told Mom or Maria about Bob's ring. I kept quiet about the silver football too. Nobody would have believed me. Had it been some sort of an airplane?

I thought about that plane I had seen yesterday. The one high above the banyan tree. Had that plane looked like a football? I couldn't be sure. But Bob had shown up again right after I saw it.

And for sure I didn't talk about Bob's home— Nrutas. His names gave me the idea to check it out. Spelled backward, Nrutas was SATURN.

Was Bob from outer space? Had he controlled that silver football? Had he planned to kidnap me? I no longer wanted to see where he lived.

And what about Angela? Had Bob tried to lure Angela away from planet Earth?

I rubbed Bob's ring. It fell into pieces like a broken

toy. And it no longer glowed. Not even when I stepped into my dark closet.

I knew then I'd never see Bob again. And I didn't want to. I knew he had never been a true friend. That made me mad. And sad too. I had really liked him.

I threw the ring pieces into the toilet. I flushed them away. Then I shuddered.

I had almost caught a kidnapper. Almost. A very strange kidnapper. People are not always what they seem to be.

I promised myself to be more cautious from now on. Caution is a good thing in a detective.

I'll never talk about this case. Not to Mom. Not to Maria. My thoughts about Bob Deed will be my special secret.

I probably just missed becoming an eponym. Drat! But there's always tomorrow.